For Jack Griffiths and Robert McLaughlin—A.D.
For Harvey—R.C.

OXFORD
UNIVERSITY PRESS

Great Clarendon Street, Oxford OX2 6DP

Oxford University Press is a department of the University of Oxford.
It furthers the University's objective of excellence in research, scholarship,
and education by publishing worldwide in

Oxford New York

Auckland Cape Town Dar es Salaam Hong Kong Karachi
Kuala Lumpur Madrid Melbourne Mexico City Nairobi
New Delhi Shanghai Taipei Toronto

With offices in
Argentina Austria Brazil Chile Czech Republic France Greece
Guatemala Hungary Italy Japan Poland Portugal Singapore
South Korea Switzerland Thailand Turkey Ukraine Vietnam

Oxford is a registered trade mark of Oxford University Press
in the UK and in certain other countries

Text © Alan Durant 2007
Illustrations © Ross Collins 2007

The moral rights of the author and illustrator have been asserted

Database right Oxford University Press (maker)

First published 2007
This paperback edition published 2008

British Library Cataloguing in Publication Data

Data available

ISBN: 978-0-19-272650-6

3 5 7 9 10 8 6 4 2

Printed in China

Paper used in the production of this book is a natural, recyclable product
made from wood grown in sustainable forests. The manufacturing process
conforms to the environmental regulations of the country of origin.

Billy Monster's Daymare

Alan Durant & Ross Collins

OXFORD
UNIVERSITY PRESS

In a darkish, creepy wood. . .

In a darkish, spooky house...

In a darkish, gloomy bedroom...

There was a...

The bedroom door creaked open.
'What's wrong, Billy Monster?' Daddy Monster
growled softly. 'Did you have a daymare?'
Billy Monster nodded. 'Yes,' he sobbed.
'I dreamt I saw a. . .

a *child*.'

'Oh dear', said Daddy Monster. 'You poor baby.' He patted Billy Monster on the head.

'It was a boy child', said Billy Monster, 'with two little eyes, and two little ears, and no horns at all!

'Ugh', snorted Daddy Monster. 'That IS horrible.'

Daddy Monster tucked in Billy
Monster again and howled a monster
lullaby until Billy Monster fell asleep.

Daddy Monster crept away, shutting the door
behind him, and went back to bed.

He had just started to burble and snore when...

'Oh, Billy,' growled Daddy Monster sleepily. 'Not another daymare?'

'Yes,' sniffed Billy Monster.

'Was it a child again?' asked Daddy Monster.

'Yes,' said Billy Monster. 'It was a girl child. She had horrible yellow hair and a tail at the back of her head. And she tried to kiss me!'

'Oh no!' cried Daddy Monster. 'That is REALLY awful. That is the worst daymare of all. You poor darling.'

Daddy Monster gave Billy Monster a cup of cold slime.
Then he stroked his horns soothingly,
until Billy Monster started to whiffle and hiss.

Daddy Monster went back to his own bed once more.
But no sooner had he started to slobber and grunt when. . .

AIIIIIEE!

'What is it now?' Daddy Monster groaned wearily.
'I think... I think... there's a child in my room,' wailed Billy Monster.
'Over there behind the curtain.' He pointed to the window
where there was a tiny gleam of daylight.
'I'll go and see,' said Daddy Monster and he pulled back the curtain.

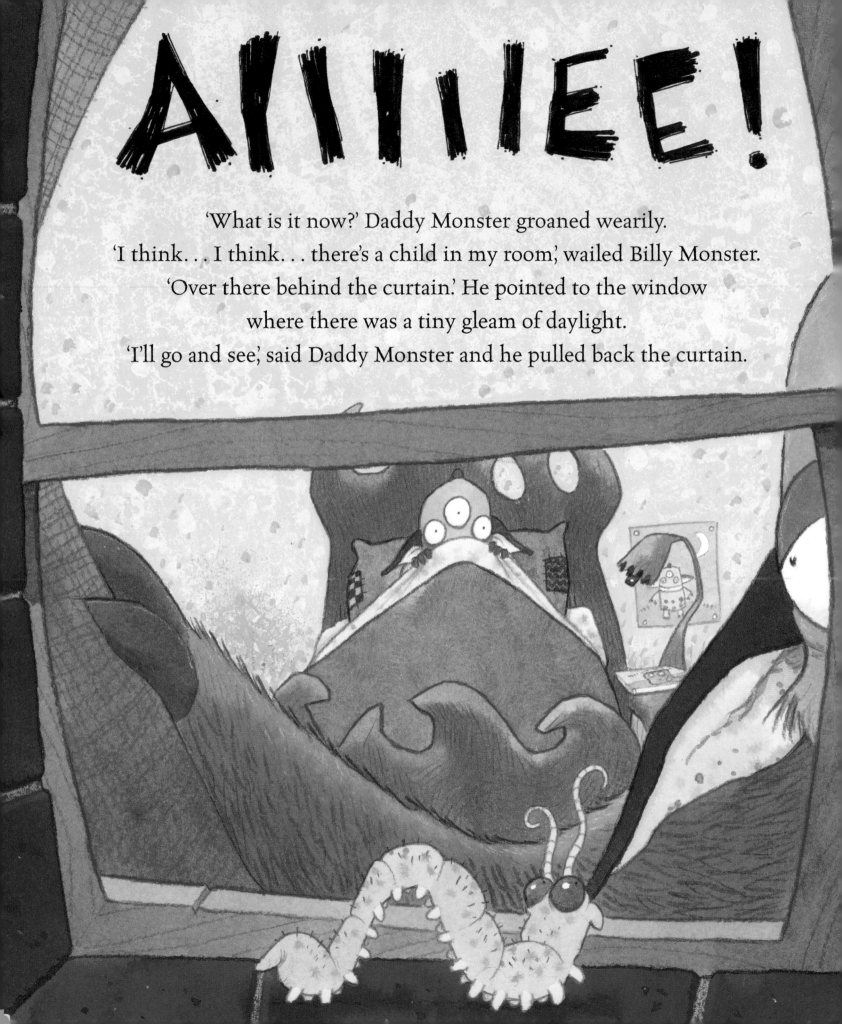

'There's no child here,' he soothed. 'See. It was just the branches of the tree you saw.' He shook his head and tutted. 'It's too light in here, that's the problem.' He drew the curtain across so that the window was completely covered. 'That's better. Now it's nice and dark.'
'Thank you,' Billy Monster breathed in a little wobbly voice.

'But. . . could you look in the cupboard too, please?'

Daddy Monster looked in the cupboard. . .

and on top of the cupboard. . .

and behind the bookcase. . .

and under the bed. . .

'See,' said Daddy Monster, 'there's no child here. There's no child anywhere, except in your head. Children aren't real.'
'Oh,' said Billy Monster. But he didn't sound very sure.
'Now, close your eyes, my little monster, and cuddle your beast,' said Daddy Monster, 'and I'll read you a lovely bedtime story.'

'Once upon a time there was a brave little monster,' Daddy Monster began.

Billy Monster sighed happily. This was his favourite story. It told how one brave little monster met some children one night and wasn't scared at all. They made friends and played spooky games together. Then they all went back to the little monster's house and ate slug and eyeball stew.

'...*And the brave little monster lived happily ever after,*' said Daddy Monster, closing the book. 'Now go to sleep, *my* brave little monster.'

Daddy Monster gave Billy Monster a big monster kiss. . .

SLUUUURRP!

Daddy Monster was just opening the bedroom door when Billy Monster
called out to him, very softly, 'Daddy Monster, well, just supposing
there was such a thing as children. . . do you think they'd have bad
dreams about monsters?'

Daddy Monster rolled
his eyes and laughed.
'Oh Billy,' he snorted,
'what a silly Billy you are! Why. . . .

who

could

scared

of

ever  be

us?'